Legacy of Love

Legacy of Love

EMILY

Anurag Anurag

Contents

1

Unspoken Connections

James Matthews was a man of routine. At forty-five, he had built a comfortable life with his wife, Linda. They lived in a quaint suburban neighborhood, where the houses were close enough to foster a sense of community but far enough to maintain privacy. James and Linda had been married for twenty years. Their relationship was built on mutual respect and companionship, though the passion that once ignited their early years had long since dimmed. They had no children, a choice they had made together, and their home was a peaceful sanctuary.

Next door lived the Bennet family. They were friendly neighbors, always ready with a wave or a cheerful greeting. The Bennets had a daughter, Emily, who had recently turned nineteen. Emily was vibrant, full of life and dreams, and her presence brought a youthful energy to the neighborhood. She was pursuing a degree in art, often seen with a sketchbook in hand, capturing the world around her with remarkable detail.

James first noticed Emily in a more profound way during one of the neighborhood gatherings. It was a sunny afternoon, and everyone was in high spirits. Emily was laughing with her friends, her joy infectious. James found himself watching her, captivated by her exuberance and the effortless way she seemed to brighten up the space around her. He quickly shook off the thought, reminding himself of his place and the life he had built.

Their initial meetings were always casual, often involving brief conversations over the garden fence or friendly exchanges when their paths crossed. James found himself looking forward to these moments, though he never admitted it to himself. There was something about Emily that drew him in – perhaps it was her passion for art, a stark contrast to his life of numbers and reports, or maybe it was simply the lightness she brought to his otherwise predictable existence.

For Emily, James was a comforting presence. He was kind and always showed genuine interest in her art. Unlike her peers, who often dismissed her aspirations as mere hobbies, James asked thoughtful questions and listened attentively. She appreciated his encouragement, and there was an unspoken understanding between them that grew with each interaction.

James's feelings for Emily crept up on him slowly, like the tide coming in. He knew it was inappropriate – he was a married man, and Emily was young enough to be his daughter. Moreover, she had a boyfriend, Tom, who was her age and seemed to make her happy. James respected this, yet he couldn't deny the flutter in his heart whenever he saw her. It was a feeling he hadn't experienced in years, and it both excited and terrified him.

The complexity of his emotions weighed heavily on James. He loved Linda, but their marriage had settled into a comfortable, if somewhat passionless, routine. The spark he felt with Emily was something he thought he had long since lost. He found himself caught in a web of guilt and longing, struggling to reconcile his feelings with his sense of duty and morality.

As the months passed, the connection between James and Emily grew stronger. It was subtle, often conveyed through lingering glances and the occasional touch that seemed to carry more meaning than words ever could. They never spoke of their feelings, but the unspoken bond was undeniable. It was as if they both understood the boundaries they couldn't cross, yet couldn't help but cherish the moments they shared.

James's internal struggle continued to intensify. He was a man who prided himself on his integrity, yet here he was, harboring feelings for a girl nearly half his age. The fear of discovery loomed over him – what would Linda think if she knew? How would the Bennets react? And most importantly, what would Emily do if he ever confessed his feelings? These questions haunted him, and he often found himself awake at night, grappling with his emotions.

Despite the turmoil within him, James couldn't bring himself to distance from Emily. Her presence had become a lifeline, a reminder that he was still capable of feeling deeply. And so, he continued to navigate the delicate balance of their unspoken connection, knowing that each encounter was a step closer to a precipice he dared not approach.

2

Growing Emotions

Over the years, James and Emily's interactions became more frequent and meaningful. Their conversations evolved from casual pleasantries to deeper discussions about life, art, and dreams. Each encounter, though brief, left a lasting impression on both of them.

James often found himself at the Bennet's house, under the pretense of discussing neighborhood matters or simply catching up. His friendship with Emily's parents, Mark and Susan, grew stronger. They appreciated his company and often invited him and Linda over for dinners and barbecues. James cherished these gatherings, not only for the camaraderie but also for the moments he could steal with Emily.

Emily, on her part, found solace in James's presence. He was unlike anyone else in her life – mature, understanding, and genuinely interested in her art. She often shared her sketches and ideas with him, and his feedback was always thoughtful and encouraging. Their bond deepened with each passing day, creating a complicated web of emotions neither of them dared to acknowledge.

One warm summer evening, the Bennets hosted a barbecue. The backyard was filled with the scent of grilled food and the sound of laughter. James was helping Mark with the grill while Linda chatted with Susan and some other neighbors. Emily was seated at a picnic table, sketching the lively scene. She looked up and caught James's eye. For a moment, everything else faded away. They exchanged a smile that spoke volumes, a silent acknowledgment of their growing connection.

As the years went by, the unspoken emotions between James and Emily became harder to ignore. James struggled with his feelings, knowing the complications they brought. His love for Linda, though different from what he felt for Emily, was still real. He was torn between the life he had built and the unexpected emotions that had blossomed within him.

Emily, too, faced her own challenges. She had a boyfriend, Tom, who was kind and supportive. Yet, there was a part of her that yearned for the connection she felt with James. She often found herself daydreaming about their conversations, replaying his words in her mind. The guilt of harboring feelings for a married man, especially one who was a friend of her parents, weighed heavily on her.

Their situation grew increasingly complex. The more they tried to maintain a façade of normalcy, the stronger their bond became. James would often stay up late, thinking about Emily, writing poems he never intended to show anyone. Emily would sketch scenes from their conversations, capturing the essence of their unspoken love in her art.

The impact of their emotions on their lives was profound. James found himself distant at times, lost in thoughts of Emily, which did not go unnoticed by Linda. She attributed his occasional detachment to work stress, unaware of the true reason. Emily's relationship with Tom also began to suffer. She became more withdrawn, her heart conflicted by her feelings for James.

One rainy afternoon, James found himself at a coffee shop, staring out the window. The sky was a melancholic gray, mirroring his mood. Emily walked in, drenched from the rain, and their eyes met. Without a word, she joined him at his table. They sat in silence for a while, the unspoken words hanging in the air between them.

"James," Emily finally said, her voice soft, "do you ever feel like there's something we're not saying?"

James looked at her, his heart aching with the weight of their shared silence. "Every day," he admitted. "But some things are too complicated to say out loud."

Emily nodded, understanding the unspoken agreement between them. They couldn't change their circumstances, but in that moment, they found comfort in each other's presence. It was a bittersweet solace, knowing that their emotions, though unspoken, were understood.

As they parted ways, the rain continued to pour, washing away the footprints they left behind. Their bond, however, remained unbroken, growing stronger with each passing day.

3

A Tragic Turn

The day began like any other. James and Linda had breakfast together, discussing mundane details of their lives. Linda had planned to visit her sister in the city, a trip she made often. She kissed James goodbye and left, promising to be back by evening. James watched her drive away, unaware that it would be the last time he saw her.

The news came in the afternoon. James was at work when his phone rang. It was a call that shattered his world.

"Mr. Matthews?" said a solemn voice on the other end. "This is Officer Greene from the city police department. I'm afraid I have some terrible news. Your wife, Linda, was involved in a car accident. She didn't make it."

The words echoed in James's mind, a cruel repetition that refused to fade. He dropped the phone, numb with disbelief. His colleagues, seeing his ashen face, rushed to his side. They spoke to him, but their words were just noise. The only thought that pierced through the haze was that Linda was gone.

James arrived at the hospital in a daze. The sight of her lifeless body broke something deep inside him. He stood there, unable to process the reality, his heart shattering with each passing second. The doctors spoke to him, explaining the details of the accident, but he couldn't focus. All he could see was Linda, motionless and serene, as if she were merely sleeping.

The days following Linda's death were a blur. James moved through them like a ghost, going through the motions but feeling nothing. The house, once a warm haven, now felt like a cold, empty shell. Everywhere he looked, he saw reminders of Linda – her favorite book on the nightstand, her slippers by the bed, the half-finished knitting project on the couch. Each reminder was a dagger to his heart, a painful reminder of the life they had shared.

Friends and neighbors came by to offer their condolences. Mark and Susan Bennet were among the first. Susan hugged James tightly, her eyes filled with tears. "James, we're so sorry," she said. "If you need anything, anything at all, we're here for you."

"Thank you," James replied, his voice barely above a whisper. He appreciated their concern but felt disconnected, as if he were watching everything from a distance.

Emily visited too. She stood awkwardly at the door, unsure of what to say. "James, I... I can't imagine what you're going through. I'm so sorry."

James looked at her, the pain in his eyes mirroring her own. "Thank you, Emily. It means a lot."

She hesitated, then stepped forward and hugged him. It was a brief, gentle embrace, but it brought a flicker of warmth to his cold heart. For a moment, he allowed himself to lean on her, to find solace in her presence.

In the weeks that followed, James tried to navigate his grief. He returned to work, hoping the routine would help him cope, but the office felt suffocating. His colleagues were kind, but their sympathy only reminded him of his loss. He often found himself staring at his computer screen, unable to concentrate, memories of Linda flooding his mind.

One evening, Emily knocked on his door. "Hey, James. I brought you some dinner. I thought you might not have the energy to cook."

James managed a small smile. "Thank you, Emily. That's very thoughtful of you."

They sat together in the living room, eating in silence. Emily could see the emptiness in his eyes, the weight of his sorrow pressing down on him.

"James, you don't have to go through this alone," she said softly. "We're all here for you."

"I know," James replied. "But it's hard. Everywhere I look, I see her. I hear her voice. I... I don't know how to move on."

Emily reached out and took his hand. "It's okay to feel that way. It's going to take time. Just know that we're here for you, whenever you need us."

Her words brought a small measure of comfort. For the first time since Linda's death, James felt a glimmer of hope, a sense that he wasn't entirely alone in his grief.

As the months passed, James slowly began to find his footing. He took up painting, something he and Linda had enjoyed together. It was a way to feel close to her, to keep her memory alive. Emily continued to visit, bringing him meals, sharing stories, and simply being there. Their bond grew stronger, a lifeline for both of them amidst the storm of grief.

But the void left by Linda's absence remained, a painful reminder of a love lost too soon. James knew he would never be the same, but he also knew that life, somehow, had to go on.

4

Silent Struggles

The days had turned into months since Linda's tragic accident, yet the ache in James's heart remained as raw as it had been the day he received the news. Each morning, he woke up to an empty bed, the silence of the house a constant reminder of his loss. Work offered little solace, and the evenings were the worst, as memories of Linda filled the empty spaces of their home.

However, amidst the grief, James found himself drawn more and more to Emily. Her visits were the few moments of light in his otherwise dark days. She had become his confidante, his anchor in a sea of sorrow. As they spent more time together, his feelings for her, which he had tried to suppress for years, grew stronger.

Emily, too, was battling her own turmoil. Her feelings for James had deepened over time, despite her relationship with Tom. There was an undeniable connection between her and James, a magnetic pull that she couldn't ignore. Yet, the societal boundaries and her loyalty to her parents kept her from voicing her true feelings.

One evening, as they sat in his living room, James felt a surge of emotion. He knew he couldn't keep it inside any longer. He needed to tell Emily how he felt. The thought had been building in his mind for weeks, and he had decided that tonight would be the night.

"Emily, can we talk?" he asked, his voice trembling slightly.

"Of course, James. What's on your mind?" she replied, looking up from her sketchbook with concern.

James took a deep breath, gathering his courage. "There's something I need to tell you. It's been weighing on me for a long time, and I can't keep it inside anymore."

Emily set her sketchbook aside, her eyes widening with curiosity and apprehension. Her heart raced, fearing what James might say. "What is it?"

James's heart pounded in his chest. He had rehearsed this moment in his mind countless times, but now that it was here, words seemed inadequate. "Emily, I—" He was interrupted by the sudden ringing of her phone.

"Sorry, let me just check this," Emily said, glancing at her phone. Her face lit up with a smile. "It's Tom. I should take this. Do you mind?"

James's heart sank, but he forced a smile. "No, go ahead."

Emily stood up and walked to the other side of the room, answering the call. As she spoke to Tom, James's mind raced. The timing couldn't have been worse. He listened to her side of the conversation, trying to decipher her emotions from her tone.

"Tom, hey! Yes, I'm at James's place... Oh, you did? That's wonderful news!... No, I haven't told anyone yet... Yes, I'll be home soon. Love you too." She hung up and turned back to James, her smile even brighter but tinged with sadness.

"Tom just proposed," she said, holding out her left hand to reveal a sparkling engagement ring. "We're engaged!"

James felt the world tilt beneath him. The words he had been about to say died in his throat. He managed a weak smile. "That's... that's wonderful news, Emily. Congratulations."

Emily beamed, but there was a flicker of something in her eyes— something that mirrored James's own hidden emotions. "Thank you, James. I'm so happy. I can't wait for you to meet him properly. You'll love him."

James nodded, struggling to maintain his composure. "I'm sure I will. You deserve all the happiness in the world."

They spent the rest of the evening discussing Emily's engagement plans, but there was an unspoken tension between them. James couldn't help but notice the way Emily's eyes lingered on him, the subtle sadness in her smile. She laughed at his jokes, but her laughter had a bittersweet edge. It was clear that she was trying to put on a brave face, but underneath, she was hurting just as much as he was.

After leaving James's house, Emily walked the short distance to her own home, each step feeling heavier than the last. She entered her quiet house, and the silence was overwhelming. As she closed the door behind her, the reality of her situation hit her like a tidal wave. She sank to the floor, tears streaming down her face. The engagement ring on her finger felt like a shackle, binding her to a future she wasn't sure she wanted.

Emily struggled to control her emotions, torn between the love she felt for Tom and the deep, unspoken connection she had with James. She thought about James's kind eyes, his supportive presence, and how he always understood her in ways no one else could. But she also thought about Tom, his unwavering support, and the stability he offered. The conflict within her was unbearable.

She cried for hours, her body shaking with sobs. The weight of her conflicting emotions crushed her, leaving her feeling lost and broken. She knew she couldn't continue like this, torn between two loves. She needed to make a decision, but every choice felt like a betrayal. Emily wanted to call James, to tell him everything, but she knew it would only make things more complicated.

As she lay on her bed, exhausted from crying, Emily whispered to herself, "What am I going to do?" She felt trapped, unable to keep her emotions for James hidden, yet equally unable to betray Tom and her family's expectations. The morning light brought little comfort, and she knew she had to find a way to move forward, despite the turmoil in her heart.

James tried to focus on work, but his thoughts kept drifting back to the previous night. His colleagues noticed his distraction and gave him sympathetic looks, thinking he was still grieving for Linda. In a way, they were right. But now, he was also mourning a love that could never be.

During lunch, his friend and colleague, Steve, sat down across from him. "You okay, James? You seem a bit off today."

James sighed. "Just a lot on my mind, I guess."

Steve nodded. "If you ever need to talk, you know I'm here, right?"

"Thanks, Steve. I appreciate it."

Later that evening, Emily called. "Hey, James. Are you free tomorrow? I'd love to have you over for dinner. Tom will be there, but I really want to see you."

James paused, sensing the underlying emotions in her voice. "Of course, Emily. I'd love to come over."

"Great," she replied, her voice softening with relief. "I'll see you tomorrow, then."

The invitation was more than just a casual dinner; it was Emily's way of trying to navigate her tumultuous feelings and the complicated bond they shared.

James's heart ached at the thought, but he knew he couldn't avoid it forever. "Sure, Emily. I'd love to."

The next evening, James found himself at Emily's house, a bottle of wine in hand. He took a deep breath before knocking on the door, steeling himself for the evening ahead. Tom greeted him with a warm smile. "James, it's great to finally meet you properly. Emily's told me so much about you."

"Likewise," James replied, forcing a smile. "Congratulations on your engagement."

"Thanks. We're really excited," Tom said, leading him inside.

Emily was in the kitchen, her face lighting up when she saw James. "Hey! Dinner's almost ready. Make yourself comfortable."

James felt a surge of conflicting emotions as he watched her. There was a warmth in her smile, but her eyes held a depth of sadness that mirrored his own. He could see the struggle behind her cheerful facade, and it took all his strength to maintain his composure.

The evening was pleasant, filled with laughter and conversation. Tom was charming and genuine, and it was clear how much he loved Emily. James found it increasingly difficult to hide his own feelings, but he did his best. Every word felt like a careful dance, avoiding the unspoken emotions that hung heavily in the air.

As the night wore on, Emily and Tom shared stories about their future plans. James listened, feeling a mix of happiness for Emily and sorrow for himself. He noticed how Emily's gaze would linger on him, her eyes filled with a wistful longing that she couldn't hide. The connection between them was palpable, but they both fought to keep their emotions in check.

"James, you should come over more often," Tom said, raising his glass. "We'd love to have you around."

James forced a smile, his heart aching. "I'd like that."

Emily looked at James, her eyes reflecting a silent plea, as if asking for his understanding and forgiveness. It was clear she was struggling with the same turmoil he felt. Their unspoken bond, though invisible to Tom, was a constant undercurrent throughout the evening.

After dinner, as they sat in the living room, James found himself watching Emily as she laughed at something Tom said. Her smile was beautiful, but there was a sadness in her eyes that only he could see. He wondered if she felt the same way he did, caught between duty and desire, love and loyalty.

Finally, as the evening drew to a close, James knew he had to leave. The emotional strain was becoming too much to bear. He stood up, forcing a light tone into his voice. "I should get going. Early workday tomorrow."

Tom clapped him on the back. "Thanks for coming, James. Let's do this again soon."

"Absolutely," James replied, his smile not quite reaching his eyes.

Emily walked him to the door, and for a brief moment, they were alone. The air between them was thick with everything they couldn't say.

"Thank you for coming," Emily whispered, her voice trembling slightly. "It means a lot to me."

James nodded, his heart breaking. "Anytime, Emily. You know I'm always here for you."

She reached out and squeezed his hand, a silent acknowledgment of their shared struggle. "Goodnight, James."

"Goodnight, Emily," he said softly, turning and walking away.

As he left, James felt the weight of their unspoken love pressing down on him. They were both trapped by their circumstances, forced to walk separate paths despite the deep connection they shared. The night air was cool, but it did little to numb the ache in his heart.

James sat in his living room, staring at the painting he had been working on. It was a landscape, but he couldn't bring himself to finish it. His thoughts were consumed by Emily and the life he would never have with her.

James picked up his phone and dialed Emily's number. She answered on the second ring, her voice immediately filling with concern. "James? Is everything okay?"

"Yeah," he replied, his voice thick with emotion. He paused, struggling to keep his feelings in check. "I just wanted to say... I'm really happy for you, Emily. You deserve all the happiness in the world."

There was a moment of silence on the other end, a silence heavy with everything left unsaid. "Thank you, James. That means a lot to me," she said softly, her voice tinged with an unspoken sadness. "You've been such a good friend. I don't know what I'd do without you."

James closed his eyes, the weight of his emotions threatening to overwhelm him. "I'm always here for you, Emily. Always."

He heard her take a shaky breath. "I know, James. I know."

After they hung up, James sat in the quiet of his living room, the silence amplifying the ache in his heart. The weight of unspoken words pressed down on him, each one a reminder of the love he could never fully express. He knew he had to move on, but it seemed impossible. The love he felt for Emily was a part of him, entwined with his very being, and letting go felt like losing another piece of his heart.

In her own home, Emily stared at her phone, tears streaming down her face. She clutched the engagement ring on her finger, torn between her commitment to Tom and the deep, unspoken bond she shared with James. The struggle within her was palpable, each breath a battle to maintain her composure. She wanted to call him back, to tell him everything, but she knew they both had to live with the choices they had made.

James threw himself into his work, trying to distract himself from the pain. He avoided social gatherings and spent most of his free time painting. It was a solitary existence, but it was the only way he knew to cope.

One evening, as he was cleaning his brushes, there was a knock on the door. He opened it to find Emily standing there, looking worried.

"James, can we talk?" she asked.

"Of course," he said, stepping aside to let her in.

They sat on the couch, an awkward silence hanging between them. Finally, Emily spoke. "I've noticed you've been avoiding me. Did I do something wrong?"

James shook his head. "No, Emily. You didn't do anything wrong. I've just been... dealing with some things."

Emily looked at him, her eyes filled with concern and something more —an unspoken longing that mirrored his own. "I miss you, James. You're my best friend, and I don't want to lose that."

James felt a lump in his throat. "I miss you too, Emily. It's just... I've been really busy with work and other stuff."

Emily's eyes widened, shimmering with unshed tears. "Oh, I see."

James took a deep breath, choosing his words carefully. "I've had a lot on my plate lately, and it's been hard to find time for everything. But I don't want you to think I'm avoiding you."'

Emily's face softened with understanding, but her eyes held a depth of emotion that words couldn't capture. "Oh, James... I had no idea."

"I know," he said, his voice steadying. "I just needed you to know that it's not about you. It's just been overwhelming."

Emily knew he was lying. She could hear it in the way his voice wavered, feel it in the unspoken tension between them. Her heart ached with the realization that James was purposefully trying to distance him-self, to protect both of them from the emotions they couldn't afford to express. She wanted to tell him she understood, that she felt the same way, but the societal boundaries and their unspoken agreement kept her silent. The pain of their mutual love, kept hidden and unspoken, was almost unbearable.

She gathered her things and made her way back home, the short walk giving her too much time to think.

As she stepped into her house, the engagement ring on her finger felt like a shackle. Her wedding was approaching fast, and while she loved Tom, her connection to James was something she couldn't ignore. The deep bond they shared, the unspoken love that lingered between them, made her heart ache with longing and regret.

Emily tried to distract herself with wedding preparations, but every detail reminded her of what she was leaving behind. She wanted to talk to someone, to share her struggle, but she knew no one would understand the depth of her emotions for James. The societal expectations, the loyalty to her parents, and the love she felt for Tom all weighed heavily on her mind.

She spent sleepless nights tossing and turning, her mind replaying moments with James, the way his eyes conveyed emotions he couldn't speak. She thought about his comforting presence, the way he always seemed to understand her without words. Each memory brought a fresh wave of tears, and she found herself questioning her choices.

"What am I going to do?" she whispered to herself in the quiet of her room, the tears flowing freely. "How can I marry Tom when I feel this way about James?"

The struggle within her was relentless, the battle between duty and desire tearing her apart. She knew she had to make a decision, but every option seemed fraught with pain and loss. Emily clung to the hope that with time, the ache in her heart would lessen, that she could find a way to move forward without losing a part of herself.

In the days leading up to her wedding, Emily continued to see James, their interactions filled with the same unspoken tension. They maintained the facade of friendship, but the depth of their feelings was always there, just beneath the surface. Each encounter left her feeling more conflicted, the love she felt for James a constant reminder of what could never be.

As her wedding day approached, Emily knew she had to find a way to reconcile her emotions. She loved Tom and wanted to build a life with him, but the connection she had with James was something she couldn't simply forget. The path ahead was uncertain, but she hoped that somehow, she could find peace with her choices and the love that lingered in her heart.

5

Separate Paths

The day of Emily's wedding arrived, a beautiful spring morning filled with the promise of new beginnings. The garden venue was adorned with flowers and twinkling lights, setting the perfect scene for a joyous occasion. Friends and family gathered, their faces glowing with happiness and anticipation.

James arrived early, taking a seat at the back, wanting to be present but not the center of attention. He watched as guests mingled and chatted, their laughter and smiles a stark contrast to the turmoil in his heart. He spotted Emily's parents, their faces radiant with pride, and felt a pang of sadness. He was genuinely happy for Emily, but the ache of unspoken love was a constant companion.

As the ceremony began, James's eyes were fixed on the aisle. When Emily appeared, her beauty took his breath away. Dressed in a flowing white gown, she looked ethereal, a vision of grace and elegance. As she walked towards Tom, her eyes briefly met James's, and in that fleeting moment, a thousand unspoken words passed between them. She gave him a small, reassuring smile, and he managed to smile back, though his heart felt heavy.

The vows were heartfelt, filled with promises of love and commitment. James listened, each word a reminder of the path Emily had chosen. As the couple exchanged rings and shared their first kiss as husband and wife, the audience erupted in applause. James clapped along, his emotions a whirlwind of joy for Emily and sorrow for himself.

During the reception, James kept a low profile, mingling with a few friends but mostly staying in the background. He watched as Emily and Tom danced, surrounded by friends and family. Their happiness was palpable, and James knew he had made the right decision in keeping his feelings to himself.

Emily approached him later in the evening, her face glowing with happiness. "Thank you for coming, James. It means a lot to me."

James smiled warmly, despite the ache in his heart. "I'm happy for you, Emily. You and Tom deserve all the happiness in the world."

She hugged him tightly, the contact brief but filled with unspoken emotions. "You've been such a good friend. I hope you know how much you mean to me."

James hugged her back, holding onto the moment. "I do, Emily. And I'm always here for you, no matter what."

As the night wore on, James decided it was time to leave. He said his goodbyes and made his way home, feeling a strange sense of closure. He had seen Emily find her happiness, and that gave him a sense of peace, even as his heart ached.

In the weeks following the wedding, James threw himself into his work, hoping to distract himself from the pain. He took on new projects and spent long hours at the office, trying to fill the void left by Emily's absence. He continued to paint, finding solace in his art, pouring his emotions onto the canvas.

Despite his efforts, thoughts of Emily were never far from his mind. He missed their conversations, the easy camaraderie they shared. Every time he saw something that reminded him of her, a pang of longing struck him. He tried to focus on the positive, reminding himself that she was happy, that she had found love with Tom.

Emily settled into her new life with Tom, adjusting to the rhythms of married life. Tom was attentive and loving, and Emily felt grateful for the stability he provided. Yet, there was a part of her heart that remained untouched, a part that still belonged to James.

She often found herself thinking about James, wondering how he was doing. The memory of his steady gaze and the warmth of his smile lingered in her mind. She missed their conversations, the unspoken understanding that had always been a part of their friendship. Despite her love for Tom, the bond she shared with James was something she couldn't easily forget.

As months passed, the distance between James and Emily grew. They saw each other less frequently, their interactions limited to occasional texts and brief conversations. Each meeting was bittersweet, filled with the same unspoken emotions. They maintained the facade of friendship, but the depth of their feelings was always there, just beneath the surface.

One afternoon, Emily called James. "Hey, James. It's been a while. How have you been?"

James felt a familiar ache at the sound of her voice. "I've been good, Emily. Busy with work. How about you?"

"Things are good," she replied, her voice softening. "I miss our talks, though. It's not the same without you."

James closed his eyes, the longing in her voice echoing his own feelings. "I miss them too, Emily. But I'm glad you're happy."

"Thanks, James. That means a lot to me," she said, her voice tinged with sadness. "Maybe we can catch up sometime?"

"I'd like that," James replied, his heart heavy with the weight of their unspoken love.

Despite the growing distance, the lingering feelings between James and Emily never truly faded. They both knew that their love for each other was something they couldn't act upon, yet it remained a constant presence in their lives. Each time they saw each other, the unspoken bond they shared was a reminder of the path not taken, the love they couldn't openly acknowledge.

James continued to paint, his work reflecting the depth of his emotions. His art became a way for him to process his feelings, to express the love he couldn't voice. Emily, too, found solace in her own creative pursuits, channeling her emotions into writing and music.

As time went on, James and Emily learned to live with their unspoken love. They found ways to move forward, to build lives that were fulfilling in their own ways. The distance between them grew, but the connection they shared remained a silent testament to the depth of their feelings.

In the end, they both understood that some loves were never meant to be fully realized. Their paths had diverged, but the bond they shared would always be a part of them. As they navigated their separate lives, they carried the memory of their unspoken love, a bittersweet reminder of what might have been.

6

A Chance Encounter

A year had passed since Emily's wedding. Life had moved forward, yet

James and Emily often found their thoughts drifting back to each other. Their busy lives kept them apart, and they gradually lost contact. Despite the distance, the unspoken bond they shared lingered, a silent echo in their hearts.

James had tried to move on, and in the process, he met Sarah, a beautiful mid-aged woman who worked as a financial planner. Sarah was intelligent, kind, and brought a sense of normalcy back into James's life. They had a comfortable relationship, yet James knew that a part of him would always belong to Emily.

Emily, on the other hand, found herself increasingly disillusioned with her marriage. The love she felt for Tom couldn't erase the deep connection she had with James. Her thoughts often wandered to James, and her heart ached with the weight of her unexpressed emotions.

One morning, James prepared for a business trip to Spain. The trip was a welcome distraction from the complexities of his emotions. As he made his way through the bustling airport, his thoughts were far from the busy surroundings. He checked in, went through security, and made his way to the gate, lost in thought.

As he approached the gate, he noticed a familiar figure standing by the window, staring out at the planes on the tarmac. His heart skipped a beat. It was Emily. She looked different, yet the same. There was a subtle sadness in her eyes, but her presence still brought a warmth to James's heart.

"Emily?" he called out, his voice a mix of surprise and joy.

Emily turned around, her eyes widening in disbelief. "James! What are you doing here?"

"I'm on a business trip to Spain," he said, smiling. "I can't believe it's you."

She smiled back, a genuine smile that lit up her face. "I'm heading to Barcelona. I'm doing a master's in ART and going as an exchange student for six months."

"That's amazing," James said, genuinely happy for her. "How have you been?"

Emily hesitated for a moment, then said, "It's been... complicated. But I'm excited about this new opportunity."

They found seats near the gate and talked about everything but their personal lives. The conversation flowed easily, as if no time had passed. They spoke about art, travel, and their current interests, avoiding the topics that could bring up their complex emotions.

"So, how's Sarah?" Emily asked, after a while, changing the subject.

James smiled. "She's great. We've been together for a few months now. She's a financial planner, very smart and driven."

Emily nodded, a flicker of something unspoken passing between them. "I'm glad you found someone, James. You deserve to be happy."

"Thank you, Emily," he replied, his voice soft. "And you? How's Tom?"

Emily's eyes clouded for a moment, but she forced a smile. "He's... fine. We're both just busy with our own lives."

James sensed the underlying tension in her words but chose not to press further. He knew there were things they both wanted to say but couldn't. The unspoken emotions hung in the air, a silent testament to their enduring connection.

The flight to Spain felt surreal. They chatted intermittently, each finding comfort in the other's presence. Upon arrival in Barcelona, they decided to spend some time together before parting ways. The city was vibrant and alive, a perfect distraction from the complexities of their emotions.

They explored the streets of Barcelona, visited art galleries, and shared meals at charming cafes. Despite the beauty around them, the unspoken tension remained. They both knew their time together was temporary, and that made each moment bittersweet.

One evening, as they sat on a terrace overlooking the city, James turned to Emily. "I'm really glad we ran into each other, Emily. It feels like old times."

Emily smiled, her eyes reflecting a mix of happiness and sorrow. "Me too, James. I've missed this. I've missed you."

They sat in silence for a moment, the weight of their emotions pressing down on them. Finally, Emily broke the silence. "I should probably go. It's getting late."

James nodded, his heart heavy. "Yeah, you're right. It's been a long day."

They walked back to their hotel, each step feeling like a countdown to their inevitable goodbye. As they reached Emily's room, she turned to face him.

"James, thank you for everything. This trip has meant more to me than you know."

James reached out and took her hand, holding it tightly. "Same here, Emily. Take care of yourself."

They stood there for a moment, their hands clasped together, the unspoken love between them palpable. Then, with a final, lingering look, they parted ways.

Over the next few months, James and Emily maintained a sporadic correspondence, their messages filled with updates on their lives and work. They avoided discussing their personal relationships, focusing instead on their shared interests and the memories they had made in Barcelona.

Despite the distance, the bond between them remained strong. They both knew that their paths had diverged, but the love they shared would always be a part of them. As they moved forward with their lives, they carried the memory of their chance encounter in Spain, a bittersweet reminder of the love that could never fully be.

James continued to build his relationship with Sarah, finding comfort and stability in her presence. Emily focused on her studies, pouring her emotions into her art. They both knew that life had a way of moving on, even when the heart struggled to keep up. And in the quiet moments, when they allowed themselves to remember, they cherished the connection that had brought them together, even if only for a brief moment in time.

7

A life Apart

After their time in Barcelona, Emily and James returned to their respective lives. The vibrant memories of their shared days lingered in their minds, casting a shadow over their routines. Despite the distance, their thoughts frequently wandered back to those precious moments.

Emily threw herself into her studies, trying to focus on her master's program in ART. She spent long hours in the studio, her emotions pouring onto the canvas. Yet, no matter how busy she was, thoughts of James were never far away. She often found herself daydreaming about their time in Barcelona, the conversations they had, and the unspoken bond they shared.

One evening, as she sat in her apartment, staring at a half-finished painting, her phone buzzed with a message from Tom. They hadn't talked much since she left for Barcelona, and the distance between them felt more significant than ever.

Tom: "Hope you're doing well. Miss you. Let's talk soon."

Emily sighed, typing a quick reply before tossing her phone aside. She knew she had to confront the issues in her marriage, but the thought of it was overwhelming. Her love for James, though unspoken, complicated everything.

Back home, James found it impossible to forget about Emily. Despite his efforts to focus on work and his relationship with Sarah, his mind kept drifting back to the time he spent with Emily in Barcelona. The connection they shared was unlike anything he had ever experienced, and it haunted him.

One evening, after another strained dinner with Sarah, James knew he couldn't continue living a lie. As they sat on the couch, Sarah sensed something was wrong.

"James, you've been distant lately. Is everything okay?" she asked, her eyes filled with concern.

James took a deep breath, his heart heavy with guilt and sadness. "Sarah, I need to be honest with you. I can't keep doing this. I've realized that my heart belongs to someone else."

Sarah's eyes welled up with tears. "Is it Emily?"

James nodded, feeling a lump in his throat. "I'm so sorry, Sarah. You deserve someone who can give you their whole heart, and I'm just not that person."

Sarah wiped her tears and nodded. "I understand, James. Thank you for being honest. I hope you find what you're looking for."

With a heavy heart, James packed his things and moved out. The breakup was painful, but he knew it was the right decision. He needed to sort out his feelings and figure out what he wanted from life.

Meanwhile, Emily continued to struggle with her emotions. Her art became an outlet for her inner turmoil, each piece reflecting the depth of her feelings for James. She tried to focus on her studies, but the longing for James was a constant presence, gnawing at her.

One night, as she worked late in the studio, her phone buzzed with a message from James.

James: "Hey Emily, how's everything going? Miss our talks."

Emily's heart skipped a beat. She stared at the message, her mind racing. She wanted to respond, to reach out and share everything she was feeling, but she knew it would only complicate things further. Instead, she typed a brief reply.

Emily: "Hey James, things are busy but good. Miss our talks too."

As she set her phone down, a tear rolled down her cheek. She knew they were both struggling with their emotions, each of them trying to navigate their lives while carrying the weight of their unspoken love. The path ahead was uncertain, but one thing was clear: they couldn't keep ignoring their feelings forever.

Emily knew she couldn't continue living in a state of emotional turmoil. The love she felt for James was too profound to ignore, and her marriage with Tom had become an unbearable facade. The internal struggle had reached a breaking point, and she realized that she had to make a change for her own sanity and happiness.

After much contemplation, Emily made the difficult decision to file for divorce. She couldn't keep pretending that everything was fine, nor could she keep lying to herself and Tom. The connection she had with James was undeniable, and it was unfair to everyone involved to keep living a lie.

With determination and a sense of clarity she hadn't felt in a long time, Emily decided she would confront James and finally confess her true feelings. She knew it wouldn't be easy, but she couldn't continue to live without acknowledging the love they shared. It was time to take a leap of faith and embrace the possibility of a future with James, regardless of the uncertainties it might bring.

40

8

Shattered Dreams

Emily arrived back home with a mix of anticipation and anxiety. Her heart was set on a new beginning, a future with James. She had made up her mind to divorce Tom, feeling that her love for James was too strong to ignore any longer. She hadn't spoken to James in a while, but the memory of their time in Barcelona and the connection they shared gave her hope.

She stepped into her home, ready to face the difficult conversations ahead. The first thing she did was to contact James, eager to share her decision and hear his voice. However, her calls went unanswered, and her messages received no reply. A sense of unease began to creep in.

Determined to see him, Emily decided to visit James's house. As she approached the familiar door, her heart pounded with a mix of excitement and nervousness. She knocked, expecting to see his welcoming smile. Instead, an unfamiliar face opened the door.

"Can I help you?" the stranger asked.

"I'm looking for James. Is he here?" Emily asked, her voice trembling slightly.

The stranger's face softened with sympathy. "I'm sorry, but James passed away a few weeks ago. He had cancer. I am his brother"

Emily felt the ground shift beneath her. "No... there must be some mistake," she whispered, her voice breaking.

The stranger shook his head. "I'm sorry. He didn't want anyone to know. He left everything in his will to someone named Emily. Is that you?"

Emily nodded, tears streaming down her face. She felt a mix of disbelief, grief, and profound sorrow. The man handed her a letter, explaining that James had left it for her.

With shaking hands, Emily opened the letter, her vision blurred by tears.

"Dear Emily,

I'm sorry I couldn't tell you this in person. I didn't want to burden you with my illness. My love for you has always been my strength, and I wanted you to remember me as I was. I've left everything to you—my house, my money, everything I have. You deserve it all and more.

Please live your life to the fullest. I will always be with you in spirit.

Love, James"

Emily clutched the letter to her chest, her sobs echoing through the empty house. The future she had envisioned with James had been cruelly taken away, leaving her world shattered. She felt a profound sense of loss, her heart heavy with the weight of unspoken words and unrealized dreams. Every unshared moment and unspoken confession now seemed like a vast chasm that could never be bridged. The plans she had silently made, the life she had hoped to build with James, were now mere fragments of a dream that would never come to pass. The grief was overwhelming, not just for the man she had lost, but for the life they could have shared, the love that had remained unspoken, and the moments that would never be. Each sob carried the weight of her sorrow, echoing through the silence of the house that now felt like a mausoleum of her lost dreams.

Returning to her house, Emily felt lost and overwhelmed. The man she loved was gone, and she was left with Tom, whom she had intended to leave. The thought of divorce now seemed uncertain. Without James, what was the point? She was trapped between the past and an uncertain future. The weight of her decisions pressed heavily on her shoulders, making each step feel like a monumental effort.

Emily wandered through her home in a daze, the familiar surroundings now alien and suffocating. Every corner of the house seemed to remind her of the life she had hoped to leave behind, while the ghost of the future she had envisioned with James haunted her relentlessly. Her heart was a battlefield of conflicting emotions: the deep, abiding love she felt for James, the lingering sense of duty and companionship she had with Tom, and the crushing grief of knowing that the man she had hoped to build a new life with was gone forever.

Sitting on the edge of her bed, Emily felt tears well up again, but she fought them back. She felt adrift, unable to find solid ground. The idea of divorcing Tom, which had once seemed like the only path to happiness, now felt meaningless and hollow. She questioned everything—her decisions, her feelings, and her future. The clarity and resolve she had felt in Barcelona had vanished, replaced by a void of uncertainty and despair.

Emily's heart ached with the realization that she was trapped, not just by her circumstances, but by her own emotions. The dreams she had nurtured were shattered, and she was left to pick up the pieces of a life that no longer made sense. She was caught between the memories of a love that would never be and the reality of a marriage that no longer fulfilled her, unsure of how to move forward.

Tom noticed her distress and tried to comfort her. "Emily, what's wrong? You've been so distant."

Emily looked at him, her eyes filled with pain. "I... I don't know, Tom. Everything has changed. I thought I knew what I wanted, but now..."

Tom held her gently, sensing the depth of her turmoil. "Whatever it is, we'll get through it together. Just tell me what's going on."

Emily shook her head, unable to find the words. She needed time to process her grief, to understand what her life would be without James. The decision to divorce Tom seemed more complicated than ever. She had to find a way to move forward, to reconcile her love for James with the reality of her life. Her mind was a tumultuous sea of emotions, each wave crashing over her, threatening to pull her under. The pain of losing James was raw and all-consuming, leaving her feeling hollow and disoriented.

She wandered aimlessly through the house, the silence almost deafening. Each room held memories of her life with Tom, now overlaid with the aching absence of James. The juxtaposition of her past and the future she had dreamed of felt like a cruel twist of fate. Her love for James had been a beacon of hope, a promise of a new beginning. Now, it felt like a distant dream, taunting her with what could never be.

Sitting down at the kitchen table, Emily buried her face in her hands. The decision to divorce Tom, once so clear, now felt like an insurmountable challenge. How could she justify ending her marriage when the person she wanted to be with was no longer there? The guilt of abandoning Tom, combined with the sorrow of losing James, created an unbearable weight on her heart.

She realized that she needed to take a step back and allow herself the time to grieve. The love she had for James was real and profound, and it deserved to be mourned properly. Only then could she begin to understand what her life could be without him. Emily knew that moving forward would require immense strength, but she was determined to find a way to honor her feelings for James while navigating the complexities of her current reality.

The path ahead was shrouded in uncertainty, but Emily resolved to face it head-on. She needed to find a way to reconcile her love for James with the life she had with Tom. It was a journey that would take time, introspection, and courage. As she wiped away her tears, Emily vowed to take it one step at a time, holding onto the memory of James as a guiding light in her search for peace and clarity.

In the quiet moments, Emily found herself talking to James as if he were still there. "I thought we had more time," she whispered into the silence, her voice breaking. "I thought we could finally be together."

Her thoughts constantly returned to the letter he had left her, reading and rereading his words. She could almost hear his voice, feel his presence, but it only made the void he left behind more profound.

One evening, She ran her fingers over the canvas of a painting he had done of her, tears streaming down her face. "Why didn't you tell me?" she cried out, her voice echoing in the emptiness. "Why didn't you let me be there for you?"

The reality of James's death forced her to confront the fragility of life and the importance of seizing the moments she had. She realized that she couldn't continue to live in limbo, caught between the past and an uncertain future. She needed to make a decision about her life with Tom, not out of obligation, but from a place of clarity and self-understanding.

Emily decided to take a leave of absence from her studies to give herself the space to grieve and heal. She spent time in nature, walking through the woods and along the beach, trying to find solace in the natural world. The sound of the waves and the rustling of leaves became her therapy, a way to connect with her emotions and start to mend her broken heart.

Slowly, she began to piece together what her future might look like. She knew that she needed to be true to herself, to honor both her love for James and the reality of her situation with Tom. It was a delicate balance, one that would require time and patience to navigate.

As she stood at the crossroads of her life, Emily resolved to move forward with intention and courage. She would carry James's memory with her, letting it guide her as she made the difficult decisions ahead. Whether it meant reconciling with Tom or forging a new path on her own, she would face the future with the strength and love that James had given her.

9

Hidden Treasures

Emily decided to visit James's home, the place that now legally belonged to her. It was a step she had been hesitant to take, fearing the flood of emotions it might unleash. But she knew she had to confront the remnants of the life James had left behind, to seek closure and perhaps find a way to move forward.

As she walked through the front door, the familiar scent of James's home enveloped her, bringing back a rush of memories. She wandered through the rooms, each one filled with his presence. The house felt eerily quiet, as if waiting for her to uncover its secrets.

In the living room, she found a large wooden chest tucked away in a corner. Curiosity piqued, she opened it, revealing hundreds of notebooks and canvases. As she carefully pulled out the first notebook and began to read, tears welled up in her eyes. James had written hundreds of beautiful poems for her, each one an intimate expression of his love.

Emily spent hours going through the notebooks, each poem more heartfelt than the last. They spoke of his love, his longing, and his dreams of a future with her. She realized how deeply he had felt for her, emotions he had kept hidden to protect their friendship and their complicated lives.

One poem read:

> *In quiet moments,*
> *I dream of you,*
> *A love so deep,*
> *so pure, so true.*
> *Yet silence holds my heart in thrall,*
> *Afraid to speak, afraid to fall.*

As she read the lines, Emily's tears flowed freely. She could feel the depth of his love and the pain of their unspoken emotions. Each poem was a testament to the love they had shared, even if it was never fully expressed.

She then turned her attention to the canvases stacked against the wall. Each painting was a masterpiece, capturing moments they had shared or images of her in different lights and moods. Some were vibrant and full of life, while others were more subdued, reflecting the complexities of their relationship.

Emily moved from one painting to the next, tracing the brushstrokes with her fingers, feeling the love and care James had poured into each piece. She spent hours immersed in his art, crying as she thought about what her life could have been if she had expressed her love to him. The paintings showed her how he had seen her—through eyes filled with love, longing, and admiration.

One painting, in particular, caught her attention. It was a portrait of her sitting by the window, lost in thought, the soft light casting a gentle glow on her face. It was a moment she remembered well, a time when they had spent an afternoon together, each lost in their own world yet deeply connected.

As the day turned into night, Emily sat surrounded by James's poems and paintings, her heart heavy with grief and regret. She thought about the life they could have shared if only she had been brave enough to express her feelings. The unspoken words, the missed opportunities, and the dreams that would never come true weighed heavily on her.

She realized that James had loved her deeply and selflessly, choosing to protect her from his illness rather than burden her with his pain. It was a testament to his character and the depth of his love. But now, she was left to navigate a world without him, carrying the weight of his unspoken love and her own regrets.

In the quiet of James's home, Emily made a vow to honor his memory by living her life fully and authentically. She would carry his love with her, letting it guide her as she faced the future. The poems and paintings were a gift, a way for her to keep a part of James with her always.

As she left James's home that night, Emily felt a sense of resolve. She knew it wouldn't be easy, but she was determined to find a way to move forward, to build a life that honored the love they had shared. And in doing so, she hoped to find peace and a way to live that would make James proud.

10

Legacy of Love

Emily spent countless hours immersed in James's poems and paintings, finding solace and connection in his art. The depth of his love and talent moved her profoundly, and she felt a renewed sense of purpose. She decided that James's work deserved to be seen by the world, not just hidden away in the confines of his home.

One evening, as she sat surrounded by his paintings, an idea sparked in her mind. She would create an Instagram account to share James's art and poetry with the world. It would be her way of honoring his memory and ensuring that his legacy lived on.

With determination, Emily set up the account, naming it "Legacy of Love." She carefully photographed each painting and transcribed his poems, posting them with heartfelt captions that conveyed the emotions behind each piece. The first post was a portrait James had painted of her, accompanied by one of his most beautiful poems.

"Through his eyes, I found myself. Through his art, I found his love. #LegacyOfLove"

At first, the account gained a modest following. Friends, family, and art enthusiasts began to like and share the posts, drawn to the raw emotion and beauty of James's work. Emily watched as the number of followers slowly grew, each new person a testament to the power of James's art.

As the weeks passed, something incredible happened. The account started gaining traction, with more and more people discovering James's work. His unique style and the deeply personal nature of his poems resonated with a wide audience. Influencers and art critics began to take notice, sharing the account with their followers and praising the profound beauty of the pieces.

One post, in particular, went viral. It was a painting of a serene landscape, paired with a poem about finding peace and love in nature. The caption read:

"In every brushstroke, he painted his heart. In every word, he penned his soul. #LegacyOfLove"

Comments flooded in, with people from all over the world expressing their admiration and gratitude for the art. Emily was overwhelmed by the response, but she felt a deep sense of fulfillment knowing that James's work was touching so many lives.

Months passed, and the account continued to grow. The follower count soared, reaching the incredible milestone of 10 million followers. James had become a posthumous sensation, his art celebrated and cherished by millions. The story of his love and talent spread far and wide, inspiring countless people.

Emily often read through the messages and comments, moved by the impact James's work had on others. People shared their own stories of love and loss, finding comfort and connection in the art and poetry. The account became a community, a place where people could come together to celebrate the beauty of love and creativity.

Sitting in James's home, now filled with the warmth of his legacy, Emily reflected on the journey they had shared. She thought about the love that had remained unspoken, the dreams that had never been realized, and the incredible impact James had left on the world. His art and poetry were a testament to the depth of his emotions and the beauty of his soul.

Emily knew that while James was gone, his love and creativity would continue to inspire and touch the hearts of many. She felt a profound sense of peace, knowing that she had played a part in preserving his legacy. Through the "Legacy of Love" account, James's work would live on, a timeless tribute to the love they had shared.

As she posted another piece of his work, Emily smiled through her tears. She knew that James was watching over her, his spirit alive in every brushstroke and every word. She whispered softly, "Thank you, James. For everything. Your love will always be a part of me."

In the quiet of James's home, surrounded by his art and poetry, Emily found solace and strength. She would carry his memory with her, letting it guide her as she moved forward. The legacy of love they had created together was a beacon of hope and inspiration, a reminder that true love never dies.

Emily found solace in her own creativity. Inspired by James's devotion and the profound impact of his art, she picked up her brushes once more. With renewed passion, she began painting again, pouring her emotions onto the canvas. She uploaded her new artwork to the same Instagram account, intertwining her creations with James's, continuing the legacy of love they had built together. Each new piece she shared was a tribute to their shared dreams and a testament to the enduring power of their connection.

As the account flourished, Emily felt a sense of peace and purpose. She realized that through her art, she could keep James's memory alive and share their story with the world. The love they had for each other transcended time and space, inspiring countless others to appreciate the beauty of love and creativity.

In the quiet moments, when she stood before a blank canvas, Emily could feel James's presence guiding her hand, encouraging her to create. She knew that he would always be with her, in every stroke of the brush and every heartfelt poem.

And so, Emily continued to paint, finding healing and hope in the legacy of love they had created. The journey was not always easy, but she faced it with the strength and courage that James had instilled in her. Through her art, she honored his memory and embraced the future, carrying forward the profound connection they had shared.

In the end, Emily understood that true love never dies. It lives on in the hearts and minds of those who remember, in the art that tells their story, and in the legacy that continues to inspire. With each new creation, she celebrated the love that had changed her life forever, knowing that James's spirit would always be a part of her.

The legacy of love they had built was a testament to the power of the human heart, a reminder that love, in all its forms, is the most beautiful and enduring creation of all. And in that legacy, Emily found her peace, her purpose, and her path forward.

The end.

www.ingramcontent.com/pod-product-compliance
Lightning Source LLC
Chambersburg PA
CBHW050617160726
48003CB00003B/1218